MOLLY, McCULLOUGH, & TOM THE ROGUE

by Kathleen Stevens   illustrated by Margot Zemach

THOMAS Y. CROWELL   NEW YORK

To Len

Text copyright © 1982 by Kathleen Stevens
Illustrations copyright © 1983 by Margot Zemach
A slightly different version of this text
first appeared in *Cricket* magazine in June 1982.
For information address Thomas Y. Crowell Junior Books,
10 East 53rd Street, New York, N.Y. 10022.
Published simultaneously in Canada by
Fitzhenry & Whiteside Limited, Toronto.
10 9 8 7 6 5 4 3 2 1
FIRST EDITION

Library of Congress Cataloging in Publication Data
Stevens, Kathleen.
    Molly, McCullough, and Tom the Rogue.

    "A slightly different version of this text
first appeared in Cricket magazine in June 1982
under the title The Rogue, McCullough, and
Molly"–T.p. verso.
    Summary: Tom Devlin roams the countryside,
charming the farmers' wives and tricking the farmers
out of fruits and vegetables, until he meets his
match in a plain-faced, sharp-tongued farmer's
daughter.
    [1. Rogues and vagabonds–Fiction.   2. Farm life
–Fiction]   I. Zemach, Margot, ill.   II. Title.
PZ7.S84454Mo 1983   [Fic]   82-45584
ISBN 0-690-04295-7
ISBN 0-690-04296-5 (lib. bdg.)

There was once a rogue named Tom Devlin who made
his living by his wits, and this was the way of it. He would
pull up his horse and cart next to a village inn. Inside,
over a mug of ale, Tom would ask the innkeeper who was
the richest farmer in the region.

Next Tom would find that farmer's land and sketch a rough map of it, with an X and the word *Treasure* marked in one corner. Then up the lane he'd ride and rap on the farmhouse door.

"Good day to you, good wife," Tom would say when the farmer's wife opened the door. "I'm a traveler with an empty stomach and tales to tell. Can you spare me a bite?" A merry grin went with his greeting, and soon Tom was seated in the kitchen, eating cold pie and telling of the curious sights he had seen.

"It's a weary life, this wandering," Tom would finish. "I'm tired of up hill and down dale, ready to build a cottage on a bit of land and raise turnips for a living." Then Tom would fold his hands over his chest and add, "On the side of a hill, perhaps," or "Next to an apple orchard sending out the scent of blossoms in May," or whatever described the land he had marked on the map.

"Why, we have a bit of land just like that!" the farmer's wife was sure to say. And charmed by Tom's fine manners and fair stories, she'd urge her husband to sell it to Tom. What with his wife coaxing and Tom jingling a bag of coins he carried in his pocket, the farmer soon struck a bargain.

Later, as the wife showed Tom the stairway to a bed in the loft, Tom would let the map fall from his pocket for the farmer to find. As Tom lay on his straw-filled mattress that night, he'd hear the farmer and his wife whispering downstairs. And the next morning the farmer would tell Tom he had changed his mind: the land was not for sale and here was Tom's money back.

Tom always acted indignant. "We struck a bargain. What will your neighbors think when they learn you're a man who goes back on his word? Perhaps we should call in the constable to settle matters." Then Tom would suggest that the farmer might prefer to give Tom something to soften the loss–a few baskets of apples or a heap of pumpkins.

The greedy farmer, anxious to be rid of Tom once and for all, would agree. And Tom would drive off to market to exchange the vegetables or fruit for a handful of silver, while the farmer and his wife rushed out to dig for a treasure that wasn't there.

One day Tom pulled up at an inn called The Three Crowns. Inside, he asked the innkeeper who was the richest farmer around. The innkeeper squinted at him. "Rich with land, or rich with happiness?"

"In my mind, it's pleasure in living that makes a man rich," Tom replied cheerfully. "But supposing I meant the first, what farmer would you name?"

"If it's wealth of land you mean, McCullough's your man," the innkeeper replied. "He's a sour fellow with grasping ways. Small wonder, living with that daughter of his. Molly McCullough is as sharp of tongue as she is plain of face. Many's the lad who has wished for McCullough's fields but balked at the thought of marrying McCullough's daughter."

Within the hour, Tom and his cart were topping the hill above McCullough's farm. The sweet smell of growing things rose on the heat of the afternoon, and for a moment Tom thought of the roots growing down into that rich soil while he was always moving on. Then he shrugged and began to sketch his map.

Soon he was knocking at the farmhouse door, ready with his smile and his stories. But the woman who opened the door gave him no answering smile. *Plain as a post,* thought Tom.

"If you're hungry, you can split wood for your supper," Molly McCullough said. And closed the door in his face.

A welcome that would sour milk! Tom noted. *If McCullough's wits are as sharp as his daughter's tongue, I must be on my mettle.* He hitched his horse to the fence and pulled his cart behind the barn. Then he turned to the woodpile. When McCullough came up from the fields, Tom greeted him, ax in hand. "Good evening, McCullough. Tom Doyle's the name. Your daughter has offered me dinner in exchange for a pile of kindling."

McCullough only grunted and went in the door, Tom close at his heels.

We're gay as a county fair around here, thought Tom, pulling out a stool at the table. "Lovely farm you've got, McCullough."

"When the locusts don't eat the crops."

Tom tried again. "Beautiful view from the hill."

"Till the fog rolls in off the river."

"Tallest corn I've ever seen."

"Dried up inside from drought."

Thoughtfully Tom wiped his plate with a bit of bread. "Delicious gravy," he said—and added before McCullough could speak, "but lumpy as week-old porridge."

Molly's eyes lighted with laughter, but her mouth stayed sternly shut. "You've had your dinner," she told Tom when she cleared away the plates.

"So I have. But I thought some tales of the sights I've seen in my travels might win me a bed for the night."

Molly tossed her head. "Words are worth nothing, and that's what you'll get for them. You can wash dishes for a night in the barn."

"Handsome offer," said Tom. "I'll wipe plates for a bed and tell stories for pleasure. My own," he added quickly.

So Molly darned socks and McCullough smoked his pipe while Tom scrubbed plates and wove tales of his travels. "It's a grand life but a weary one," he finished. "I'm thinking how fine it must be to settle down and work the soil. Perhaps, McCullough, you'd have a bit of land I could buy for a cottage and a patch of vegetables? By a bend in the river, perhaps, with a willow to shade my front door."

McCullough took his pipe from his mouth. "How much?"

Tom reached into his pocket. As he pulled out the pouch of coins, the map fluttered to the floor. McCullough's eyes narrowed, but he never mentioned it. He weighed the pouch, then agreed to sell Tom the land he had described.

As he left for the barn, Tom saw McCullough scoop up the map. Walking through the moonlight, Tom sang to himself, "Hey-a-down-derry! Tomorrow McCullough's vegetables will line my pockets with silver."

The next morning Molly was nowhere in sight. But sure enough, McCullough wanted his land back. Tom, of course, protested loudly. At last McCullough offered Tom a sack of cabbages to make up for his disappointment.

"One sack of cabbages for the loss of a man's dream?" Tom shook his head.

Long they haggled, with Tom determined to drive a hard bargain and McCullough not giving an inch. Finally McCullough said, "Here's my last offer. The sacks filled with cabbages are piled beside the corncrib. You can take as many sacks as you can carry away."

"Done!" cried Tom. He ran behind the barn and dragged out his cart.

McCullough's eyes widened as Tom swung one lumpy sack after another onto the cart until not a sack was left. Then Tom turned with a grin. "My thanks for your cabbages and a grand day to you, McCullough." Hitching up his horse, he leaped onto the cart and set off up the lane.

From the hilltop, Tom looked back. McCullough was headed for the river, a shovel in his hand. "Oh, McCullough," Tom said with a shake of his head as he stopped the cart. "The ground of your farm is filled with a treasure richer than any map could bring you. That's a lovely bit of land down by the willow. I wonder if I made a mistake giving it up for a cartload of cabbages."

"Especially these cabbages," came a voice from the back of the cart.

"What?" cried Tom. "Cabbages that talk?" He turned to the nearest sack and pulled it open. Inside was a heap of straw and stones. "I've been cheated!" roared Tom.

"Why not?" said the same voice. "One good trick deserves another."

"Straw and stones talk no more than cabbages," Tom said grimly. "Whose voice speaks from these sacks?"

"Tear out the cord and you'll see." And one sack began to move.

When Tom ripped it open, up rose Molly McCullough.

Tom's face reddened. "I've been played the fool. McCullough promised me cabbages. He gave me straw and a woman prickly as a hedgehog."

"You gave him a map for a treasure that does not exist. The bargain was evenly matched." Molly McCullough planted her hands on her hips. "But you can still get a piece of his farm now and all of it later."

Tom threw back his head in scorn. "The only way to do that is to marry his daughter—a shrew with a tongue sharp as a sickle!"

Now it was Molly who flushed with anger. Tom held up his hand. "I only repeat what they say in The Three Crowns."

"Stupid men merit sharp tongues," snapped Molly. "I've saved my soft words for a man clever enough to deserve them."

"So," said Tom thoughtfully. "But there's another problem. No man willingly chooses a woman without beauty."

Molly's chin tilted. "If your eyes are so dull they see beauty only on the outside, you are less clever than I thought."

Tom scratched his chin. "I've long been a wandering man, living by my wits…"

"Cheating honest farmers!" Molly put in.

"Not so honest that they ever pointed out the map I dropped on the floor," Tom retorted. "Be that as it may, I like the idea of putting down roots and using my back along with my brains. I will return to McCullough and ask for the hand of his daughter."

A smile stole across Molly's face. *Ah,* thought Tom, *my eyes were dull indeed when they failed to see the softness a smile would work in that face.*

Molly climbed up beside him, and Tom turned the cart around. Said Tom with a chuckle, "McCullough will be angry with me—he's dug all this time and found nothing. On the other hand, I have a right to a bit of temper over the trick he played me."

Molly folded her hands in her lap. "My father thinks he gave you cabbages. It was I who put straw and stones in the sacks."

"What?" Looking at Molly, Tom roared with laughter. "You're a bigger rogue than both of us, lass. To think that I have been outsmarted by a woman!"

Smooth as fresh cream came the voice of Molly McCullough. "Perhaps for the first time, my Thomas. But certainly not for the last."

Still laughing, Tom clucked to his horse, and the wagon bumped down the lane, with Tom and Molly side by side on the wooden seat.